SONATINA IN F

for Treble Recorder (or Flute) and Piano

ROBIN MILFORD

I

Duration : 6½ minutes

Oxford University Press 1958

Printed in Great Britain

OXFORD UNIVERSITY PRESS, MUSIC DEPARTMENT, GREAT CLARENDON STREET, OXFORD OX2 6DP

★Fingerings for
A♯ B♮ & C♯ D♯ trills

Sonatina in F

4

Sonatina in **F**

II

Sonatina in F

III

Vivo (non troppo)

Sonatina in F

II

Andante

III

(senza rit.)

Sonatina in F

OXFORD UNIVERSITY PRESS

SONATINA IN F

for Treble Recorder (or Flute) and Piano

Treble Recorder (or Flute)

ROBIN MILFORD

I

Duration: 6½ minutes

★Fingerings for
A♯ B♮ & C♯ D♯ trills

Sonatina in F

Sonatina in F

Sonatina in F

Processed and printed by
Halstan & Co. Ltd., Amersham, Bucks., England

Sonatina in F

OXFORD UNIVERSITY PRESS